DISCARDED

The Carrot Seed

by **RUTH KRAUSS**

Pictures by **CROCKETT JOHNSON**

SCHOLASTIC INC.
New York Toronto London Auckland Sydney

No part of this publication may be reproduced in whole or in part, or stored in a retrieval system, or transmitted in any form or by any means, electronic, mechanical, photocopying, recording, or otherwise, without written permission of the publisher. For information regarding permission, write to Harper & Row, Publishers, Inc., 10 East 53rd Street, New York, NY 10022.

ISBN 0-590-00386-0

Copyright 1945 by Ruth Krauss and Crockett Johnson. This edition is published by Scholastic Inc., 730 Broadway, New York, NY 10003, by arrangement with Harper & Row, Publishers, Inc.

80 79 78 77 76 75   10 11 12/0

Printed in the U.S.A.   08

A little boy planted
a carrot seed.

His mother said, "I'm afraid
it won't come up."

His father said, "I'm afraid
it won't come up."

And his big brother said,
"It won't come up."

Every day the little boy
pulled up the weeds around the seed
and sprinkled the ground with water.

But nothing came up.

And nothing came up.

Everyone kept saying
it wouldn't come up.

But he still pulled up
the weeds around it every day
and sprinkled the ground with water.

And then, one day,

a carrot came up

just as the little boy

had known it would.